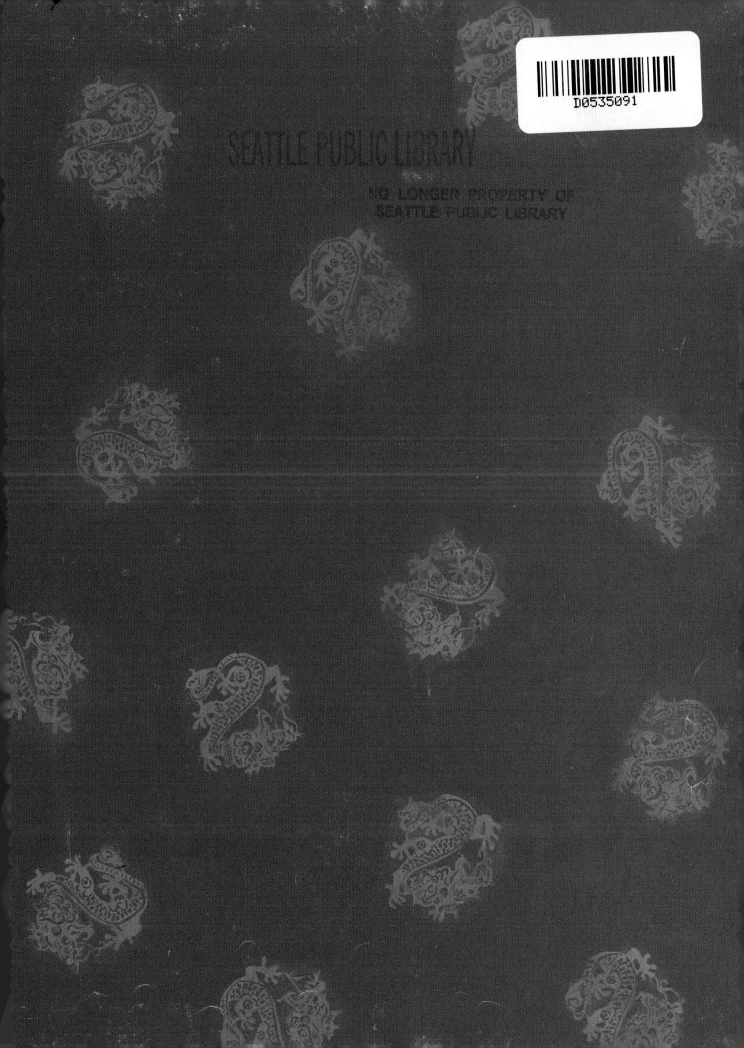

Sanne te Loo

# Ping-Li's  Kite

FRONT STREET & LEMNISCAAT Asheville, North Carolina

Ping-Li wanted to make a kite that
would fly higher and be bolder
than any kite he had ever seen.

So he went to Mr. Fo's shop
for paper, sticks,
and string.

"But," Mr. Fo warned him,

"you must paint your kite before you fly it

or the emperor of the sky will be angry."

After he left the store, Ping-Li
sat on the temple steps
and built his kite.

On the way home, Ping-Li couldn't
resist flying his unpainted kite.
He dreamed that his kite
would be the best of all.

While Ping-Li slept, the emperor of the sky
swooped down in his dragonship and
plucked the kite from the air.

"Your kite is the most boring kite in the sky!"
the emperor yelled.
"Come up here, now!"

Ping-Li climbed to the dragonship.

"You must make your kite
better than all the kites in my ship!"
the emperor commanded.

So Ping-Li began to paint...

and the emperor

smiled at Ping-Li's kite,

which flew higher and was bolder than
any other kite in the sky.